There I Am

by Debi Famelos

Illustrated by: Jessica Szaszi

Balboa Press books may be ordered through booksellers or by contacting:

Balboa Press
A Division of Hay House
1663 Liberty Drive
Bloomington, IN 47403
www.balboapress.com
844-682-1282

Interior Image Credit: Jessica Szaszi

ISBN: 978-1-9822-6097-2 (sc)
ISBN: 978-1-9822-6096-5 (e)

Print information available on the last page.

Balboa Press rev. date: 01/20/2021

BALBOA.PRESS
A DIVISION OF HAY HOUSE

To:
From:

Life is full of sweetness when
we see ourselves in others.

Celebrate the
Sameness
in all Beings

Jai Jamelos
H

Dedication

To my beautiful children and grandchildren.

Extraordinary "Beings" whose endless curiosity for observing the world unveils this truth:

"Everywhere I go, everyone I see, is a reflection of myself, a little part of me."

Let's look closely together
now and very soon we'll know,

that we're a part
of everyone
everywhere we go.

When I look into
the mirror myself
looks back at me.

I am a beautiful one of a kind, myself is all I see.

Yet when I look out into the world
and see all the life out there…

I begin to see we're all
alike, there's something
special we all share.

I watch them go about
their lives and I can see
they're all beautiful too.

Yet I notice something very cool,
they express all the things I do!

It's more then our beautiful eyes and smiles.

It's more then whether we have legs or arms...

It's that we are "Being" the same is so many ways.

It's our natural "Being" charm.

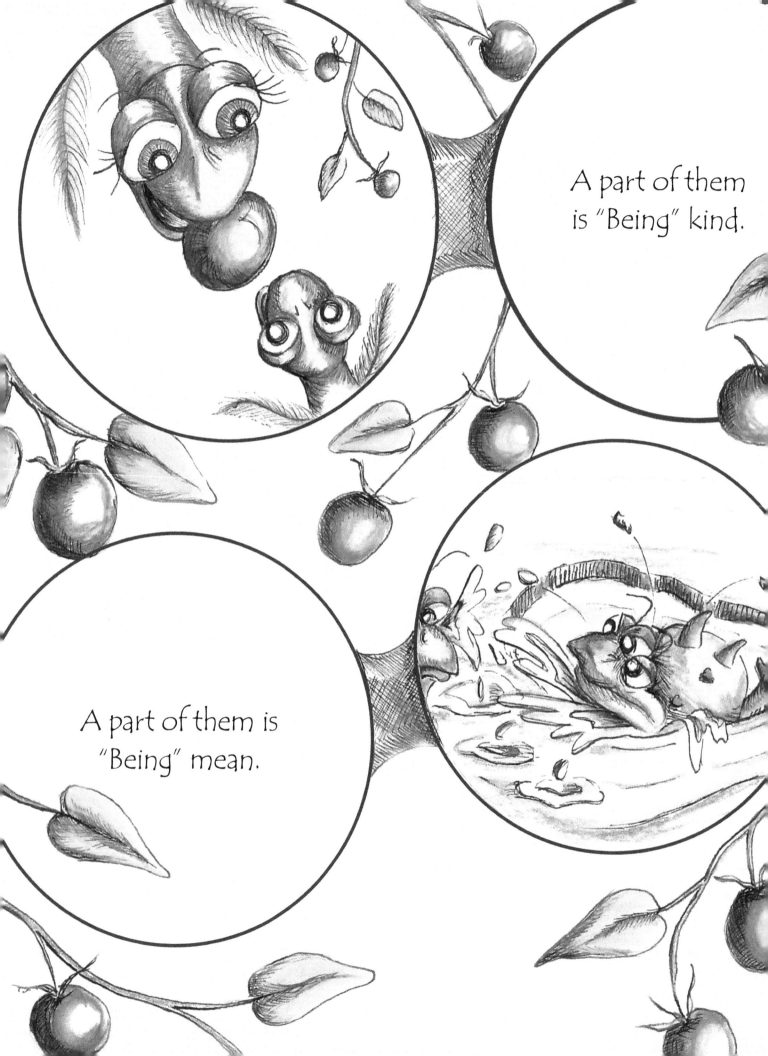

A part of them is "Being" kind.

A part of them is "Being" mean.

I try to "Be" a friend.
The best friend
you've ever seen!

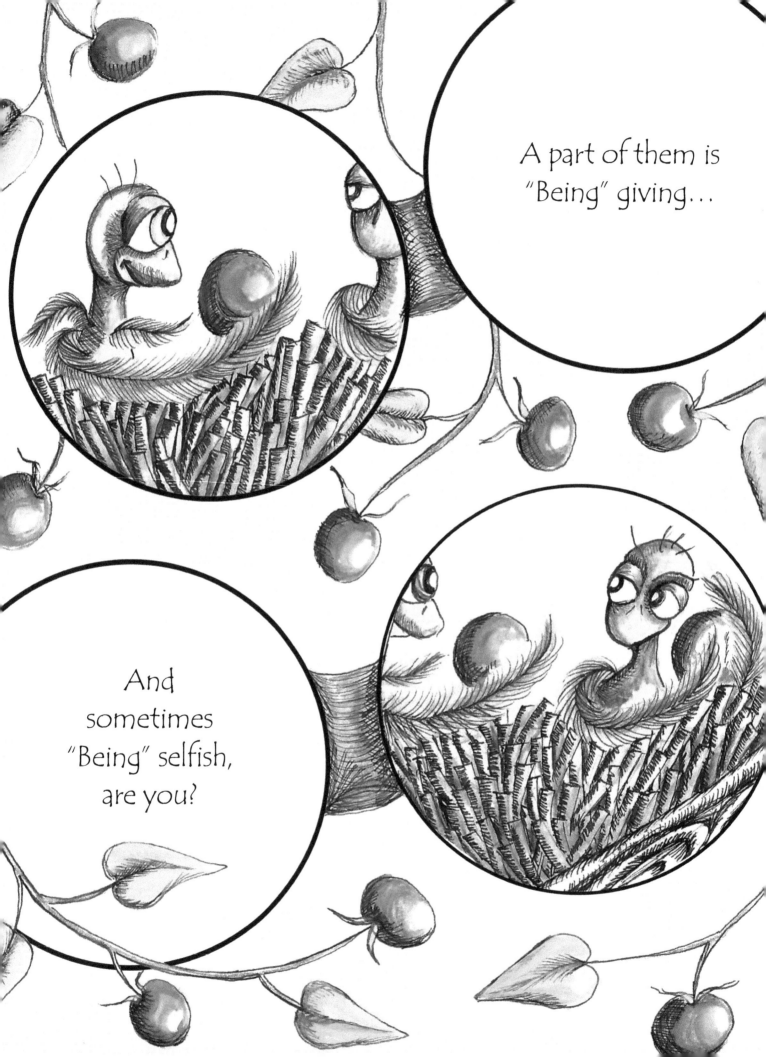

A part of them is "Being" giving…

And sometimes "Being" selfish, are you?

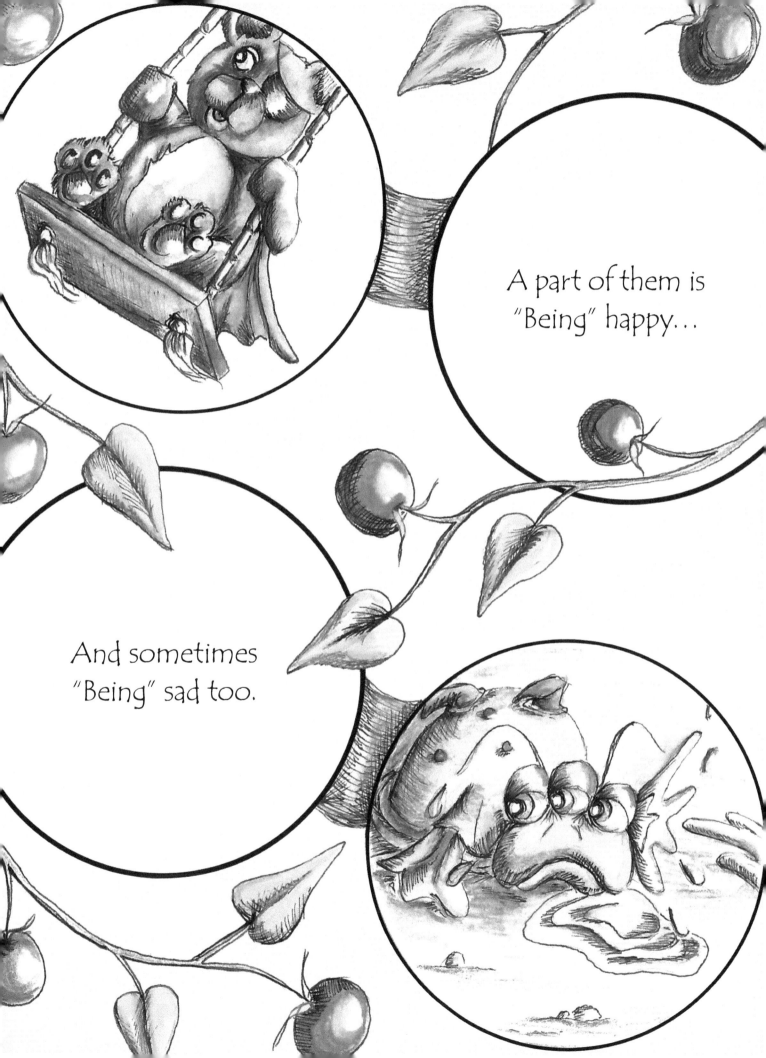

A part of them is
"Being" happy...

And sometimes
"Being" sad too.

I know that I too am
all these things.

There's not one among us who
escapes any of these "Beings".

So now I know wherever I go,

And know whoever I see…

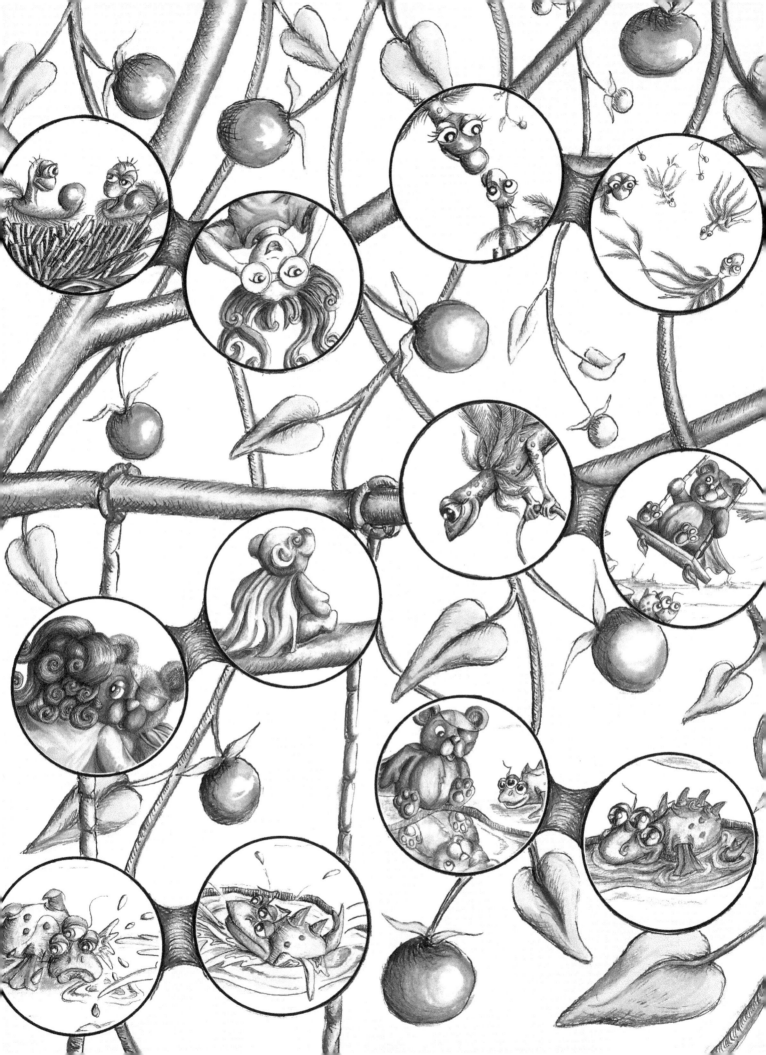

CPSIA information can be obtained
at www.ICGtesting.com
Printed in the USA
BVHW022258250121
598391BV00003B/4